SCORPION TALES

S D JOHNSON

Cover photo by Kelsey Dody on Unsplash.

❀ Created with Vellum

FOREWORD

This collection of short stories is characterised by variety of style and genre. They include historically factual tales, historical fiction, murder stories, stories of obsession and tales of the ordinary.

They have one thing in common. There is always a sting in the tale.

Demons and Charade are correct in their historical content. In all of the other short stories, all characters and events are fictional and in no way reference real people or events.

DEMONS

February 21st, 1921.
Brno, Czechoslovakia.

I had stopped for the night in the small village of Brno and had found lodgings in what appeared to be its only inn. I had stowed my bag in the room and come downstairs to take advantage of the fire in the bar.

"He drinks the profits," the old man at the only table said, nodding at the innkeeper. "He'll drink himself to death. Haunted, he is, and drowning in debt."

I looked more closely at the owner of the inn. He was a shrivelled-looking man, slightly hunched at the shoulders and with eyes that looked as if they had peered at the gates of hell and were terrified of returning and stepping through them.

"That your car?" he asked, peering out of the window into the dusk at my Austin 20, my one possession and my only means of trying to keep myself one step ahead of my demons. I nodded and the old man at the bar glanced at me and raised his brows knowingly and rolled his eyes.

"Not much of a car, is it?" he said, graciousness was not

one of his priorities.

"It does its job," I replied, not wanting to get myself into an argument.

"I used to drive a Graf and Stift," he said, as if I should know immediately the significance of that. "I was a chauffeur to royalty in that beauty. Mind you, that was just for the one day, but it was a day that changed my life, I can tell you."

I was there for the night, I was in no hurry to retreat to my nightmares in my cold and sparse room, and the bar was warm and comforting. I ordered another beer and prepared myself to hear his tale, which the old man had clearly heard too many times. He looked at me as if to say he had warned me and drained his glass.

"Royalty, you say?" I asked. "King George?"

He laughed, but the laughter was bitter. "You British, you think you rule the world! You and your beloved king emperor. Let me tell you, I worked that day for the heir to the greatest empire the world ever knew: the Austro-Hungarian Empire. What do you say to that?"

I had nothing to say, but, as I had no wish to leave the warmth of the bar, I said politely, "That must have been quite a day for you."

He threw his head back and roared with hollow laughter. "For me, you say. For the world, I say."

He came from behind the bar and settled into the leather armchair by the fire with a very large drink and nodded for me to join him on the opposite seat. The old man from the table nodded farewell and left.

"It was June," he said, "a beautiful, sunny day. My boss and I picked them up at the station in Sarajevo. They were friends of his, you see, and he was out to gain favour, so he put me and the car at their disposal."

"Who was your boss?"

He looked irritated. "Count Harrach", he replied, but I

was none the wiser. I realised he expected me to let him tell his story uninterrupted.

"They were going to inspect the troops up at the garrison. He was a major general, you see, as well as heir to the empire, and that rank entitled them both to be on public display on big military occasions. He wanted to give his wife some lime-light since the royal family refused to acknowledge her. They didn't think she was good enough for him, poor woman, but he was besotted."

He paused to take a long drink from his glass before continuing. "The crowds were about eight deep as we drove along Appel Quay. They were cheering and waving and the two of them were lapping it up. They were all lovey-dovey, it was their wedding anniversary you see, and they loved all the attention." You could see from his expression that he was back there, able to see the images and hear the sounds of that day.

I was still not sure who they were, but the unfolding story offered more cheer than that spartan room upstairs and the horrors of the night, so I nodded enthusiastically, and he went on.

"All of a sudden there was one hell of a bang on the bonnet. Damn me, it was a hand grenade, so I swerved, and it bounced off and blew up the car behind. The two in that car really caught it, and it took out about twenty of the crowd as well. There was smoke and screaming and blood everywhere."

"We drove like hell to the Governor's residence and he was flaming mad when he got there. He let them have it, I can tell you. Stupid man, he'd known all along that there was likely to be an attempt on his life, but he'd ignored all the warnings. He wanted to give her the royal pomp and glory treatment. Then they decided, all regal-like, to go to the hospital to visit the wounded, but, typical, they didn't tell us drivers, so off we went on the original route to the garrison." He took another large swig from his glass.

"We turned off Appel Quay as planned, and the official in the car starts shouting at me to stop and go back, so I slammed the brakes on. As soon as we stopped, I put the car in reverse and, would you believe it, I stalled it. I swear to God, I never stalled any car before, and then, there he was, the little shit, Gavrilo Princip, standing there with his Browning in his hand, and he fired two shots. The first got her, and the other got him." He paused to refill his glass.

"They reckon they called him Gavrilo after the Archangel Gabriel: more like the Angel of bleeding Death. Only nineteen he was, and there he was, calm as you like: just shot two people in front of witnesses, trying to take his cyanide pill like it's a mint humbug or something, but they got him."

The story was starting to make connections in my exhausted brain, dulled after that day's drive of eight hours. This man, this innkeeper, with his sallow skin and tormented eyes was a major player in world history. I felt my stomach churn as I looked at him.

"You were driving the Archduke Ferdinand and his wife when they were shot?" I asked.

"Of course I was," he said. "Who did you think I was driving? The Emperor of bleeding China? Yes, I'm Leopold Lojka," he said, "the bringer of war." He laughed, but there was no humour there.

This man had set the history of the twentieth century on its bloody course just by taking a wrong turn and stalling a car. If he hadn't taken the wrong turn, if he hadn't stalled the car, then Princip would have just gone home. Instead, my host had delivered the Archduke Ferdinand straight to the barrel of Princip's Browning automatic. I had to hear the end of his story, this little man, whose accidental stalling of a car had changed the history of the world.

"Do you know, they made me send telegrams of apology. I had to send one to the Emperor Franz Josef, one to Kaiser Bill and one to their children, as if it was my fault they got shot." He shook his head. "Anyway, when the old man, Franz Josef, died and the Emperor Charles took over, he went and gave me 400,000 crowns, didn't he? Made me take the blame they did, but Charlie, God bless him, he tried to see me right. I set myself up in this place and, d'you know, I've lost just about every single crown. I'm cursed. No matter what I do, I'm cursed." He lapsed into his own thoughts.

"What happened to Princip?" I asked, trying to give him some relief from that painful reverie.

"They put him on trial. I had to give evidence for the prosecution. Do you know, he was just 27 days too young for the death penalty? Not that it did him any good, he got 20 years solitary, but he went and got TB and died."

He stood up, shook his head and poured us both another drink. He returned, clearly back in the present once more. "You want to see Franz Ferdinand's braces? I've got them behind the bar, still covered in his blood, though that's gone brown now. I got a bit of her bracelet, too: Sophie her name was." He got them from below the counter and handed them to me.

And there I stood, history in my hands and in the presence of this tortured man who had set the great conflict, the so-called war to end all wars, in motion.

I went to bed and slept soundly for the first time in years. I'd met a man whose demons were so infinitely greater than my own that perspective could finally enter my head. Yes, I had the images of the trenches seared on my brain, but this man had lit the torch that set the world on fire when he stalled that car. He had to live each day with the deaths of millions weighing upon his soul.

THE STING

*H*e grabbed her jaw and jerked her head viciously towards the light, checking the camouflage of her make up over the angry bruise on her cheek bone. He released it roughly, satisfied that the disguise was as good as she could make it.

With a sigh, Jay went to put on her coat and shoes ready to leave for her morning in town.

"What are you messing about at?" he shouted to her, "You'll miss your bus."

Satisfied that she had done everything, she left the flat. She was meticulous on her trips to town. Every minute had to be accounted for, so she always made sure her trail was easy to follow.

She sat next to Mavis Dean on the bus. Mavis was in her eighties and as sharp as a pin. If he asked her, she'd be able to tell him that they'd had a nice chat. The stench of dried urine from Mavis almost took Jay's breath away, but it was worth it to have a firm alibi.

She did most of her shopping on the market. Not for her the anonymity of the self-service points in the supermarket.

She had to go where people knew them both, and make sure she chatted as she shopped.

"You been bumping into doors again?" the woman on the veg stall asked, peering at her face.

"Something like that," Jay replied, hoping that the woman would let it drop, and praying she would never mention it to him.

He wanted his shoes soling and heeling and she had twenty blissful minutes to sit with a cappuccino in the café opposite the shoe stall whilst they were done. It was rare that she got to have a coffee, because these minutes would be largely unaccounted for when she related her doings on her return home. The smell of that cappuccino was an absolute delight and she savoured every drop, remembering to suck a mint afterwards to erase the smell, and checking her coat for tell-tale drips. She knew how careful she had to be.

She went into the bank to withdraw cash. He didn't trust ATMs and counter withdrawals would come with a receipt with the time printed on it. She checked the receipt for their balance: that piece of information could not be denied her. It was as low as usual, indicating he had had no luck on the horses that week.

The bus journey home was tricky because she didn't recognise anyone to sit next to, but thankfully bumped into their neighbour as she got off the bus. She could have cried with relief when the neighbour asked her what time it was. If he ever asked, that would be watertight.

She could hear the radio as she unlocked the door to the flat; it was deafeningly loud. She flinched out of the way as a wasp flew past her towards the light from the open door.

So, she was ready for whatever he asked of her, and she had completed all the errands on budget and exactly as stipulated. What would he be able to find fault with this time.

He would never find fault with her again. He was

slumped in his chair, bulging eyes staring blankly at the ceiling, tongue grossly swollen filling up the whole of his open mouth. In his lifeless hand was clutched his Epi-pen. She didn't know if he'd used it or if it had failed to work. What she did know was that he was dead, never to raise a hand to her again, and she felt cold with shock and horror.

Should she ask for an ambulance? He was clearly dead. She didn't know what to do, so she dialled 999 and let them advise her. Then she dialled his brother, Joe, and asked him to come round straight away. Then she sat on the stairs to wait, and tears ran down her face faster than she could wipe them away.

Joe got there before the emergency services and, after absorbing the news, took command. He was not at all like his brother, and he could see his sister-in-law was in a total state of shock and distress.

The days that followed were all a bit of a blur for Jay. She could not stand to be in the flat, she could not get the sight of him out of her mind, so she stayed with her sister. It felt so strange to be allowed to spend time together, but these were chilling circumstances and she largely wanted to be alone and be silent.

She thanked God for his Peter, his brother, who took care of all the arrangements. He dealt with the police, the inquest, arranged the funeral and sorted out all the paperwork. Things dragged on because there had to be a post mortem and so it was nearly five weeks before they could lay him to rest. They were dreadful weeks, with life held in limbo, but she held on tight and got through them as best she could.

The post mortem had confirmed he had died of anaphylaxis after receiving repeated wasp stings. He had used his Epi-pen but it had been ineffective against the severity of the stings. Peter was able to protect her from most of the legal matters and logistics, but he could not protect her from the funeral. She had to attend.

He had arranged for the cortege to leave from their family home, and collected Jay and her sister on the morning of the funeral. The hearse and car were already parked outside and so they transferred directly to the funeral car.

They made a forlorn little group: Jay and her sister, Peter and his wife and his widowed mother. There were mourners already waiting at the church, largely his work colleagues, his drinking friends and his gambling mates and they followed the family party in in silence.

Jay never could recall a word of that service. It was simply a blur of mumbled hymns, mumbled prayers and a jumble of words in the eulogy from an anonymous vicar that could have applied to anyone.

What did stay in her mind were words spoken to her at the graveside as they walked away, leaving him in the open grave. It was not the ubiquitous, empty condolences from people unknown to her, but the words from his mother and brother. Both hugged her tightly.

"He never deserved you," Peter said.

"You deserved better, my girl," his mother said.

Inevitably it was time to move on, but where to and how were not clear to Jay. She gave notice on the flat and, having removed her things, Peter emptied his belongings and left it ready for the landlord to let to the next tenant. She eventually found courage to rent an apartment in Cartagena in Southern Spain. She needed time to heal and time to think.

The sun was kind to her and her bruises healed more quickly than she expected. It bronzed her skin lightly, and put highlights in her previously mousey hair. It felt wonderful to wear a sundress, and feel the warmth on her arms and shoulders, and to wear sandals and see the pearly pink varnish on her toes. She read her way through the selection of books she had bought at the airport and generally relaxed and learned to breathe again.

Most precious were the coffees she drank in the open-air cafes, enjoying the freedom to linger over her drink and even ordering a second one if she felt like it. She was sitting reading and enjoying a coffee after a long walk along the harbour front when she felt a light touch on her arm.

"Do you speak English?" an elderly lady enquired.

She smiled, "I am English," she replied.

"There's a wasp sitting on your pastry," the woman said, "Be careful you don't get stung."

"Let him enjoy it," Jay said, "It's pay-back time."

The woman looked puzzled, clearly having no idea what Jay meant.

"I used to be cruel to wasps. I used to catch them in the garden and keep them in jam jars until they got really angry." The woman was looking at her as if she were crazy. "I always released them, just as I was leaving home," she said in her defence, although the woman had stopped listening.

They were right, Jay decided, all those wise people who said that confession was good for the soul.

TRUST SHATTERED

*B*rian did not hide his irritation when Helen reminded him that Jules and David were coming to dinner. He pulled on his tatty walking coat, clipped the lead on to the dog's collar and disappeared. She knew he would be missing for a couple of hours.

Brian: kind, quiet, dependable, slightly autistic, super-intelligent Brian. She had felt secure in his love for her from the day they met and it was his steadfastness and strength that had helped her through the pain of their four still-born babies.

Anyway, if Brian was down, she had the evening with Jules and Dave to look forward to. They brought fun and chaos wherever they went. They had only married just over a year before, though they had been together for fifteen years. Their wedding had been a riot, and she and Jules planned every detail. Jules was never going to be traditional and the two of them had shopped for weeks to find the perfect outfit: best described as wafting poet meets Karma Chameleon.

Dinner at Jules and David's house was always unpredictable. They had once sat on cushions and shared a sumptuous Moroccan feast, although she and Brain could not be persuaded to try the hookah pipe. On another occasion they had been fed on mung bean and quinoa curry, followed by a basil and lentil ice cream. Once they had been plied with fish finger sandwiches laced with Ketchup, and a Wagon Wheel for dessert: that was when Jules cooked what was alleged to be an ironic menu. Helen's menu was safe and reliable, and she had bought in ample stocks of wine.

Brian's walk had not lifted his mood and even the dog was subdued when they returned. Brian retreated to the shed to "mend something." That was what he did for pleasure. He would buy unloved and damaged goods from car boot sales and flea markets and spend hours tinkering with them, restoring them and upcycling them.

Helen wrote stories for women's magazines. Her earnings varied, but were sufficient to supplement Brian's income as a chemical engineer. She relied heavily on Jules and David for companionship; the sort that Brian could not provide. Jules was her shopping buddy: her provider of fun and gossip. They went to outrageously expensive shops, where the Prosecco was uncorked on their arrival. She noted Jules's glass was always well-filled and kept refreshed, whereas she was proffered a glass largely containing bubbles. She had no complaints: she spent nothing, whereas Jules's platinum card regularly glowed with white heat.

David was her culture partner. Jules liked the theatre, but really had a taste limited only to musicals and thrillers so Helen went with David to operas, ballets and concerts and they argued over poetry and novels during the intervals. They enjoyed a meeting of minds and relished their debates.

Brian was Brian, and she truly believed that all three of them recognised his goodness, respected his intellect and integrity and loved him just as he was. He accepted her need to spend time with each of them, and always seemed happy to be the quiet part of their monthly meals together. That was what made his reaction that evening so unusual: he really was not happy.

She had to fetch him from his shed so he could shower and change. Brian always wore shirts, ties and V-necked pullovers. He never looked sharp or smart, he just looked creased and comfortable, just the way she loved him, and so he looked just the same, but cleaner and tidier.

She thought Jules and David were not as bright as usual. She knew David was waiting for a call-back for a part in a new drama series, which was unusual for him, so thought that was troubling him. He was normally offered roles without an audition: perhaps he was worried that his star was beginning to wane, although he and Jules had no need to worry financially: the royalties from his voice overs and repeat fees kept them in the luxuries they both craved.

Brian was silent during the meal and picked at his food with disinterest. Jules and David drank more than usual, sniped at each other endlessly and were louder than normal, and, untypically, unfunny. Helen did her best to keep them in harmony around her table. She usually loved it when the four of them sat around it in candlelight, sharing stories and memories and dissolving into gales of laughter. It wasn't working, and it was clear that David was getting deliberately drunk rather than mellow and merry. He followed her into the kitchen and watched her as she brewed their coffee, cup by cup, in the neat little machine.

"I feel sorry for you, Helen," he said.

Oh God, she hoped he was not going to bring up her four lost babies. He would never have done this normally, unless she talked about them, but tonight he was drunk and there was a bitter edge to him.

"No need," she said brightly, "I'm perfectly content."

"You wouldn't be if you knew," he said, and he clearly wanted her to pursue the matter.

"Go on then, David," she said, "since you clearly want to tell me."

"Jules and Brian have been having an affair," he said.

It was so ridiculous that she laughed and picked up the tray of cups but as she turned, she saw Brian ashen faced in the doorway.

"How did you know?" Brian asked, and she knew, in that instant that David was telling the truth. She put down the tray and both she and Brian stared at David, waiting for an answer.

"Because I bet the silly old tart a Caribbean Christmas if he could seduce Brian," he said bitterly, "and he's only gone and done it."

There was a deathly pause, each one aware of their heart pounding so loud it echoed in their ears.

At last, Helen broke the silence. "I think you'd better leave," she said.

THE FAN

*M*rs. Burton had taken to her bed with a fever. Her elder daughter and both her sons were staying with her sister in Bath, and her younger daughter, Alexandra, was being particularly stubborn.

"Mama, why may I not go to the ball with the Crewes?"

Mrs. Burton's head throbbed and she wanted the interview concluded. She knew by continuing to deny her daughter permission to attend the ball she succeeded only in lengthening the debate: Lexie could be most single-minded.

"I will speak to your father."

Lexie knew she had won. Indeed, she had: later, her father pronounced the Crewes a most suitable family and decreed that Lexie should go to the ball with them and then stay over with them until the following day.

Mrs. Burton and her husband had very different views on suitability and she knew very well that Mrs. Crewe would be gossiping all evening and would leave the young ladies to their own devices, but her fever grew worse and she had no energy to protest further.

· · ·

LEXIE AND ELIZA CREWE were alight with excitement on the day of the ball and practised endlessly how they would engage with the young gentlemen there. They rehearsed with great diligence how they would peep over their fans, and then avert their eyes and retreat behind them when noticed.

They practised their most demure smiles, following the smile with an immediate flick of the fan and a subterfuge of coyness. They deemed themselves most accomplished at the art of feminine flirtation.

MRS. BURTON WAS QUITE CORRECT: as soon as they arrived at the ball, Mrs. Crewe joined the small

coterie of her most intimate acquaintances and quite forgot her promise to never for one minute take her eyes off those darling girls.

Those darling girls linked arms and promenaded around the room, locked in conversation yet ever

surveying the assembly for young gentlemen. Their tinkling laughter might have been thought excessive by some. Certainly, Mrs. Burton would have had them sit by her side and stop making a show of themselves, but she was some miles away, languishing on her pillows and powerless to intervene.

"Oh do look, Lexie. That very tall gentleman is looking our way."

Both girls looked at him with interest from behind their fans. He looked most distinguished, and

was in the company of a Mr. Davenport, who Eliza declared to be the most admirable and wealthy

young man of the neighbourhood. He returned their look with confidence, and both girls bestowed upon him their most feminine smiles before hiding their blushes behind their fans.

"Oh Lexie, they are both coming over," Eliza was fluttering her fan quite rapidly.

"Miss Eliza," said Mr. Davenport. "May I present my friend, Mr. Edward Dunwoody?"

Both girls dropped a curtsey and the tall man bowed in response.

"Delighted, sir," said Eliza. "This is my friend, Miss Lexie Burton." Both gentlemen inclined their

heads in acknowledgment.

The gentlemen wondered if the young ladies would care to take some refreshments, which, of

course, they did, and so the four retreated to the adjoining room where the gentlemen acquired

glasses of Canary for them all.

The dancing had begun and both girls were most anxious to join in and the gentlemen were only

too happy to oblige. They all proved themselves adept at the quadrille and the reels and

Lexie felt herself very grown-up as she and Mr. Dunwoody progressed down the set. She felt they were quite the most handsome couple in the room and she was sure the young ladies sitting alongside their mamas, as she knew she should have been, would be most envious.

"Excellent, excellent," declared Mr. Davenport, as the set concluded.

All four were a little flushed after their exertions and all agreed that more Canary was called for.

"Miss Lexie, I fear you have over-exerted yourself. Perhaps you might like to take a turn in the

garden with me?"

"I'm sure Lexie is absolutely fine," said Eliza, who was slightly more aware of the habits of young

gentlemen than her more sheltered friend. She, after all,

had circulated the local balls unfettered by the watchfulness of her mother for some months.

Lexie was most impressed by Mr. Dunwoody's concern for her well-being and had long dreamed of being the object of a gentleman's attentions.

"It is a little chilly outside, Dunwoody, " remarked Mr. Davenport, who was well aware of his friend's

inclinations and was sensitive to Eliza's tender age and innocence.

"I'm sure a little fresh air would be just the thing to restore me," Eliza said, blithely oblivious to the

discreet concerns of the other two, and most anxious to secure more of the delightful attention of Mr. Dunwoody.

Dunwoody extended his arm, Lexie placed her hand on it in what she hoped was a seemly but assured manner, and together they stepped through the open doors into the night air. She hoped she disguised the involuntary shiver as the chill met her arms.

The garden was lit by torches and lanterns and the paths encircled fountains and rose beds, and

Dunwoody led her to the flower bed and picked a rose for her.

"Your hand is so cold," he said, encircling it in his own.

That gesture was so delightful to Lexie. She smelled the heady scent of the rose and sighed with happiness, unaware that they no longer kept to the paths but now found themselves concealed behind a ponderous oak tree.

Lexie had learnt to turn and twist to escape her two brothers' teasing and wrestling and she

unexpectedly found she needed all those skills to free herself from Edward Dunwoody's hands, which were suddenly exploring places that she had previously no idea were of interest to gentlemen. She landed a deft kick on his shin, twisted quickly and pulled herself free.

"You minx," he said bitterly. "Flutter your fan at some other fool, but waste no more of your

teasing on me." He strode off angrily toward the house, leaving her to smooth her hair, adjust her

gown and feel the full force of the mortification of her foolishness engulf her.

She took some minutes to regain her composure before returning to the house and took a seat

at Mrs. Crewe's side. Mrs. Crewe nodded acknowledgment without registering the young girls'

flushed face or tearful eyes. Eliza Crewe was too busy dancing with Mr. Davenport to notice the distress of her friend, and Lexie felt no urge to enlighten her then, or when they returned to the Crewe's home later that night.

Lexie was exceedingly glad to return to her own home, relieved to find her mother much improved and was thankful to return that hateful fan back into its box.

THE FAN MMXX

*J*oe Tate was in a hurry and he decided to leave through the club to save a couple of minutes. It was just his bad luck that the owner's wife called him over. He joined her at the bar, where she was working on her lap top.

"My daughter, Lexie, is quite a fan of yours," she said, barely raising her eyes from the screen.

"That's nice," he said, at a loss as to where the conversation was going.

"She wants to take some pictures at your next gig for her photography project," she raised her eyes and looked directly at him, knowing this would be the last thing he would want.

"Difficult one, this", he thought. He could visualise her daughter, he often caught sight of her as he went out each day: she'd waiting for one of her parents and would be sitting at a table doing her schoolwork or reading. She was privately educated, and appeared regularly with her pony tail neatly brushed, wearing her lilac tartan pleated skirt and her purple school blazer. He could imagine her at the Wednesday gig, girly and giggly, annoying his usual crowd.

"No offence, but it wouldn't be right," he said.

"And why's that?"

"The Wednesday crowd can be tough, no place for a schoolgirl with her Barbie camera," he replied, aware he wasn't expressing himself well, but trying to make his point.

"Obviously, she wouldn't be wearing her uniform," the woman said. "And as my husband owns this club, pays your wages and rents you your flat, it seems to me that you will say yes. She'll see you ten or fifteen minutes before you go on stage so you can talk things through. I'll be sitting towards the back keeping an eye on her." Her eyes shifted back to the screen; the conversation was over.

He turned his back abruptly and went into the street annoyed, bitterly regretting taking that short cut. He did not notice her, Lexie, that day, sitting in the corner, her head down over her school books, apparently oblivious to everything around her.

On the Wednesday evening, she duly arrived fifteen minutes before he was due to start his set. He was astonished; she certainly wouldn't have been taken for her schoolgirl that night: she looked like the kind of girl he would never have plucked up the courage to approach. She was classy, poised and very self-composed. She was toting some very impressive Pentax kit, and looked totally at ease with it. He had to gather himself very quickly and focus as she began to speak.

She explained the shots she wanted, working on her assumptions about where he would be standing during his set. She spoke of the angles she was aiming for, and where she would position herself. She was confident and had clearly thought out the shoot with care.

"This is so good of you," she ended, with a disarming smile. "I think my mother told you I'm a fan of your music. Thank you for letting me do this."

He nodded like an idiot, "No problem. Glad to help. You just do what you have to."

"I'll share the pictures with you. If you like them, you can use them on your website," she said. "I haven't moved on to my business model yet so I won't charge."

TWO DAYS later an envelope was delivered through his letterbox. There were fifty shots on a memory stick: each shot exceeded his wildest expectations. She had captured the very essence of his performance: the energy, the emotion and the atmosphere were all there in every shot. She had used her talent to capture his passion for his music in a series of dynamic images. There was also a note with her email address, asking him for feedback.

He replied straight away.

Hi Lexie,

Your pictures are brilliant. I will def. be using them on my website.

You are amazing.

Cheers and thanks,

Joe.

He didn't hear from her again but he loaded the shots on his website, carried on promoting his YouTube channel and working the clubs and the student bars. Things were starting to look up: he was starting to earn from the advertising on YouTube and the hits were rising daily. His Twitter account was busier than ever, his number of followers on Facebook was growing and he'd got some interest from the local radio station and TV station.

HE OPENED his door some five weeks later without a worry

in his mind. He was taken aback to be faced by two detectives.

It all happened so fast from then. His laptop, his mobile and his computer were seized and he was in custody facing a list of charges of sexual offences against a juvenile.

The evidence was overwhelming.

The photographs on his laptop and computer were conclusive: lewd and explicit pictures of Lexie had been taken in his flat. She was pictured in his bed, in his shower, sprawled across the kitchen table, leaning over the kitchen stools and in each picture, there she was, always looking scared, with those terrified blue eyes staring into the camera.

The forensic evidence that had been captured throughout the flat was particularly compelling. Her DNA was present everywhere, even on his laundry in the washing basket.

The emails had been sent from an untraced pay-as-you-go mobile. They were damning in their demands of her: their detail was graphic and their perversion grotesque.

He never stood a chance. She was brilliant in the witness box, dignified but clearly deeply damaged by it all, and it took only thirty minutes for the jury to reach their guilty verdict. When he was sentenced, she looked him straight in the eyes and never flinched or showed the slightest emotion.

She had needed the assistance of her father's duplicate keys to his flat; a zoom lens; the timer on her camera; a tripod; latex gloves for wearing when downloading images on to his computers; the diligence to adjust the time and reset it each time she used them; a pay-as-you go mobile phone and an email address set up in his name that he would claim to have no knowledge of, and, above all, her confidence in the boring routine of his daily movements. This had allowed her to access his rooms after school. The phone, which now lay, minus sim-card, at the bottom of the canal, was used to send the emails from the very locations he visited regularly.

She had taught him the cost of disrespecting a fan. She had also taught him what a schoolgirl fan with sufficient determination can accomplish.

BEING BRIAN

I always liked Brian. He was a polite lad and, whilst he kept a low profile in class, he would always venture an answer when asked.

He was never going to be popular with his peers. For a start, his name echoed of the past. He had elderly parents: lovely people, very supportive but so old-fashioned in their ways. Everything about him reflected their values, so he was always immaculately dressed.

The sharp centre crease in his trousers made him stand apart from the other lads, whose trousers never saw an iron. He wore a green V-necked sweater in both winter and summer, showing off a perfectly tied tie. The other lads just wore their white shirts, usually out at the waist, with their ties hung defiantly low and loose.

His shoes were sturdy black lace ups. They were always immaculately polished. The other lads wore black leather trainers, usually muddy and scuffed.

Brian was different but was never bullied. The lads just left him alone. At break and lunchtime they would tear off to the fields and play football, keeping their game alive as long after the bell as they could. Brian would be in the computer room or in the library, helping the elderly librarian stack books on the high shelves.

His loneliness was most noticeable in the dining room. He would come in late, after most of the kids had left, and collect his food and sit alone.

If I happened to be in the dining room at the same time, I would sit with him whilst I ate my lunch. It didn't happen very often, but when it did, we would chat away.

I can't remember specifically what we talked about; it would mostly be about how he was getting on in school. He was a diligent student and he constantly strived to get into the top sets, but he never quite made it, always hovering near the top in the second sets.

It was during one of these conversations that he announced that he had taken up the piano. He had found a teacher near to where his grandma lived, so he would go to his lessons whilst his parents visited the elderly lady.

From then on, I always remembered to ask how he was getting on with his piano lessons. The lad got really interested in it and was excited by his progress. He had found something he was good at.

Within the year, he told me that he was on grade 6 and that he had been asked to play in Nottinghamshire's Arts Festival, his grandma's county, because that's where he had his lessons.

By the next Christmas he told me that he was at Grade 8 and would be auditioning for the Musical Maestro television show, where all the contestants were under eighteen. It was very popular with the kids at that time as the winner the previous year had gone on to world wide chart success as a solo artist. At Easter, he told me he had been selected.

I was pleased for the lad. He didn't go around boasting. I don't think anyone else in the school knew, and he preferred it that way. He just seemed content that I was following his musical career and taking notice of him.

At a staff meeting we were discussing how we should acknowledge our students' achievements more widely. Various kids were mentioned, but they were all well known to us and had had plenty of recognition, and we wanted someone who was under the radar at that time so I mentioned Brian and his forthcoming appearance on TV.

The other teachers were genuinely thrilled to hear that such a nice, modest, almost invisible young lad was doing so well, and so he became the student whose profile we needed to raise.

I did question if this was wise. He was so modest I wondered if it would embarrass him. It was decided that he would receive the major award in our achievement assembly, only if he agreed to the public recognition.

He did agree, rather more eagerly than I expected. The other kids were amazed when they found out that Brian was going to be on TV on such a popular program, and they cheered and cheered and stamped their feet. It wasn't that they had disliked him before, they had just never noticed him.

Brian had never had a reaction like it and he blushed as he retook his seat with his trophy in hand. That day the other kids acknowledged him as they passed him in the corridors. It was only a grunted "Aw-right Bri," but it was more than he'd ever had before, and it felt good.

I was pleased to see that none of this went to his head, and he remained the same modest young man. One lunchtime when we had a chat, he mentioned that filming was starting that weekend. It was good to see him with such a clear focus.

I met his parents at the Year 10 Parents' Evening. They were as delightful as ever and thanked me profusely for the interest I took in their boy. They said it made a tremendous difference to his confidence. Like all teachers, I appreciated their thanks. It is a job that seems to bring an endless stream of complaints and thanks are rare.

"I'm sure you're very proud of him," I said.

"We are," they nodded. "He always does his best."

"About his piano playing, I mean."

They looked perplexed.

"He's done so well at his grades. He really has some determination," I clarified.

"Brian doesn't play the piano," his mum said.

My heart started to pound.

"He's never touched a piano in his life," his dad said.

Very quietly, I explained what had happened in school. They knew nothing of it. He hadn't taken his trophy home.

I could see the disappointment seeping into them as they discovered that their boy was a liar. I tried to put it into context, aware that I was the sole architect of his fall from grace. He had only ever told me. It had been me who had spread the word.

" I'll talk it over with my senior colleagues. I'm sure they'll want to involve you in how we handle this. How you deal with it at home is entirely up to you."

They thanked me and left without keeping their appointments with his other teachers.

I may have been a little cavalier in nominating him, but Brian must have had his reasons for confiding his tale to me and would doubtless suffer anguish when his parents confronted him.

That night I was left to confront my conscience. I had created this whole problem. I hadn't even checked his story; I'd taken it at face value. Looking back, that was so naive of me. It stood to reason his success would have been picked up by the local papers or local radio.

The next day I talked it over with the pastoral head and I owned up to my own lack of responsibility over the matter. Together we decided to ask the student welfare manager to seek an educational psychologist's appointment for Brian. For Brian's sake, we would let him permeate the story that he'd withdrawn from the TV show because of the pressure of his GCSEs. We invited his parents in and they agreed with our course of action.

The school had a very clear anti-bullying policy and staff were active as soon as the trouble started. We stuck to the script in school about Brian withdrawing but somehow word got out that he didn't actually play the piano. Maybe his parents had confided in someone, because Brian would not have told a soul. He was too mortified.

"Brian the Liar" started to appear on lavatory doors, penned in an ugly scrawl.

He was pushed and bumped into in corridors whenever there was the opportunity to do so unobserved.

He had been left alone before, totally ignored, but now he wasn't just left alone, he was stared at, pointed at, laughed at and ridiculed wherever he went.

It was worse for him at the start of lessons, when the kids entered the classroom and there were a couple of minutes before the teacher arrived. The they had free rein and kids can be very cruel.

I sat with him at lunchtime when I could. He had already apologised to me for lying and I had admitted that I should have checked it out before I made it public. It was odd. There was a deep sadness about him, his eyes were red and there was always a sigh in his voice when he spoke. To give him credit, he was never reproachful to me but always rather shamefaced.

One day he looked at me sadly and said, "Sir, I just want it all to stop,"

"Give it time, Brian. There will soon be something else for them to concentrate on. There always is." I could offer no other comfort.

That day I was due to cover his class's Geography lesson. I was about four minutes late as it was quite a distance from the Science block where I taught to the Humanities block.

As I got nearer, kids were running past me screaming. A cold certainty enveloped me, and I started to run.

Brian emerged from the classroom, a vicious kitchen knife in his hand, dripping with blood. His face and hands were smeared and, from behind the door I could hear groaning.

"I told you sir," he said. "I told you I wanted it to stop."

This time there was unmistakable reproach in his voice.

CHARADE

"*P*eople are so stupid," Claude said.

There was no one there to hear her but her hunting hound, but Claude preferred his company to most humans. She brushed her short hair roughly, her lips tightly compressed.

"And you, Robert des Armoises, are the most stupid man I ever met," she said, flinging her brush down.

That was hardly fair to the man who had married her, the knight from one of the oldest families in France, who had brought her to his manor and wanted to treat her like a great lady. What he wanted and what he could afford were two very different things and this was the cause of much discontent for Claude. There were no lady's maids or fine trappings for Claude.

"Why did you let me go to Orléans? Why couldn't you have been man enough to forbid me to go?"

Again, it was hardly fair. She would have gone, no matter what. It was also two months since her disastrous visit to Orléans and she was still blaming him.

It had been she who had cropped her hair again, found

out her gentleman's outfits and brushed them down, and taken off to Orleans to indulge herself once again in her fantasy.

It had worked. As soon as she got there she was recognised, and there were celebrations and lavish gifts and she had revelled in the attention.

It was just sheer chance and bad luck that Jean Luilier, Joan's tailor, had been right next to her at the last reception and had accidentally taken the wine glass meant for her. In the confusion, as he returned the glass to her, he looked closely at her, and she saw the beginning of a glimmer of realisation in his eyes.

She had rushed out of the reception that night in panic and fled home. The knowledge that she had come so close to being discovered had thrown her into terror.

It had all been so easy in the beginning. She had let four years pass before she thought it was safe to begin her deceit. She had worked at her credibility and posed as a soldier and fought for the pope in Rome in 1435, killing two men and establishing herself as a worthy warrior.

She had then hooked up with Pierre and Jean, Joan's brothers. They were stupid too. To that day, she truly didn't know if they believed she was their sister, but the three of them had had a fine time playing make-believe for the whole of 1436. They had toured the North East of France with their charade and had been lavishly entertained and showered with gifts.

Their best time of all had been in Arlon. The three had become favourites of the Princess Elizabeth de Luxembourg and Duchess Elisabeth von Görlitz. It was in Arlon, under their patronage, that she had acquired her lasting taste for luxury and comfort.

That was what made her life there in the manor, with the

stink of the animals in the yard creeping in through every door and window, so unbearable.

The rushes on the floor were not changed regularly, her husband had to exercise thrift, so the stench lingered and clung to her clothes, which were not the fine silks loaned to her by her hostesses in Arlon, but the simple woollen weave of the countryside.

And then there were her sons. She had had two boys in two years: howling, screaming brats who the nurse seemed unable to pacify. True, she did not see them often, but their howls echoed through the house night and day and made her head throb.

The time in Arlon had been the best in her life until that stupid man had been fully taken in, and had fallen in love with her. The Comte de Virnenbourg was entertaining and generous at first, but then he had become enchanted by Joan's legend. He put her, Claude, in charge of a military unit and despatched her to Cologne to support his man for the bishopric of Trier.

Stupid man. She only wanted to be feted and spoilt, she certainly didn't want to be his diplomat, but his purse was too generous and too tempting for her to refuse so she had gone.

To be honest, she knew she would be a disaster as a diplomat. She liked to drink, and she loved the company of men. Both these things could embolden her and made her reckless.

She had a repertoire of tricks and illusions and, when she was carousing and the drink had taken hold, she had entertained her adoring audience. Word spread, and the Inquisitor began to suspect her of witchcraft.

Things got difficult for her. In the end, she had to send word to the Comte to rescue her. He sent men and got her away just before the Inquisitor's guards arrived to arrest her. The Inquisitor excommunicated her in absentia for witchcraft, for wearing men's clothes and for supporting the wrong candidate for the bishopric.

She did not actually care because it was Joan he excommunicated, not her, Claude. She did care that her life of luxury was over.

She never saw the brothers again. They had scuttled off to safety. She had let the Comte down and was out of favour with him and also with both the duchess and the princess. This was why she had set her cap at Jean des Armoises, the knight from the countryside who was paying a brief visit to Arlon.

Her charms had worked, and they had married swiftly. He was twenty years older than her, not rich enough for her tastes and somewhat vulgar and earthy in his habits, despite his excellent family pedigree, but he was the best option that was available.

Times were hard for him. The wars with the English had led to high taxes and his wealth had been depleted. Yields were low and labour was more or less impossible to find. So many local men had lost their lives in the war, and the able bodied of those who remained had become his tenants. Peasantry was becoming a thing of the past in France, far quicker than in the rest of Europe.

True, they paid rent, but he could not afford a manager and every week he would have to spend a full day out on his horse, collecting their money. At harvest time he had no choice but to labour in the fields alongside what crew he could bring together.

Sometimes she sensed he had grown weary of her, but she could still exercise her sexual wiles on him and, in general, he was fairly compliant.

She had always been convinced of his stupidity. He knew, as did all of France, that Joan had been burned at the stake in Rouen in 1431. The English had not just burned her once.

They had raked over her ashes twice and set them alight again each time. They had then thrown the final sweepings into the Seine. She was as sure as she could be that he believed that his young wife, Claude, was, in fact, the resurrected Maid of Orléans.

She had pondered all this that morning. The morning that the messenger arrived from the king, along with four guards.

Charles VII had finally heard about her exploits in Orléans, and, anxious to meet this girl, summoned her to the palace.

She was thrown into a panic. Jean Luilier had scared her, made her fear for her safety, and he was only a tailor. Now she had to take her charade to the palace and meet the king. She didn't even know what he looked like, and she was supposed to be the one who crowned him.

When the king commanded, his subjects had to obey without question, and so she got out her gentleman's clothes and made herself ready.

On the way, she made good use of her womanly skills and elicited from the messenger that Charles had a very sore, ulcerated foot and had taken to wearing a soft leather shoe. She also learned of the possibility that she might be presented to someone posing as the king.

Her bravado had never been as tested as it was as she strode into the court that day. She had become accustomed to pomp and finery at Arlon, but that did not prepare her for the opulence of the French court. The ladies, with their steeple hats and fine silks, stared at her with undisguised curiosity as she made her entrance.

She scanned the men in the room as she walked down the pathway that had been created as the throng had parted, checking their feet for mismatching shoes.

At length she detected a soft leather shoe alongside a

finely embroidered one and, ignoring the imposing figure standing alone at the head of the crowd who appeared to be waiting for her, threw herself at the oddly shod feet.

"Sire," she said, and her forehead touched the ground.

"Joan," the king said, stretching his hand to hers and holding it whilst she rose to her feet. He wrapped her in a tight embrace.

Her pounding heart slowed its beat a little and she found it easier to get air into her tightened chest.

"Come," he said, taking her hand again. "We must talk", and he led her towards a separate chamber off the great hall.

He waved all attendants away, sat himself on an opulent chaise, and nodded for her to sit in the chair opposite him.

"Now we can talk at last about that secret known only by you and me," and he smiled, and in that moment, in that smile, she saw that he knew and that her charade was finally over.

"They all believe," he said quietly, "because they want to believe. We two know the truth."

JEAN

*T*he run up to Christmas was always hectic for Jean. In that last week alone, she had been busy from morning to night every single day. If she was honest, she was exhausted. She wasn't getting any younger and her arthritis gave her jip in the cold weather.

On Monday the Luncheon Club Christmas Lunch she had organised for the elderly members at the garden centre had been really successful. The minibuses had been on time, the food was excellent, everyone had received a gift, provided by the garden centre and wrapped by her, and they had all been in good spirits.

On Tuesday she had driven round the various participating shops to collect the Christmas shoe boxes, filled with items for the Romanian orphans, that they had been collecting. She had then taken them all to the collection depot in town and had spent the afternoon helping to sort them into separate piles for boys and girls, and then packing them into the larger boxes for transportation.

She had got up early on Wednesday morning to bake mince pies for the WI cake stall and had helped to man their stall during the afternoon at the festival of carols at the local hospice.

On Thursday she had done her regular day at the charity shop in the village, standing outside for a good few hours selling raffle tickets. The footfall in the shop had been really poor that day and the manageress wanted to give ticket sales a boost. She'd then driven into town to do the early stint on the Soup Run.

On Friday she had baked more mince pies and had taken them to the Memory Café's Christmas tea and had spent the afternoon serving cups of tea and sitting chatting to the carers and the members. The entertainment she had organised was particularly good. The local minstrels' group had come along and sang songs from yesteryear and everyone had joined in. There had been loads of washing up, but she didn't mind because the company was good.

She had made it to Christmas Eve. Her shopping was done, and she had locked her front door and poured herself a glass of the sherry she had won at the hospice raffle. Time to put her feet up and watch the soaps she'd missed that week on catch-up TV.

Her doorbell rang. It was her neighbour, Eileen.

"Hello Jean. Sid and I were wondering if you could come round tomorrow lunch time," Eileen said.

"I'd love to," Jean's face beamed. Her heart soared. Someone wanted her.

"If you can just let the dog out for ten minutes, we'd be ever so grateful," Eileen said. "We're at our Linda's for the day."

IN CONTROL

"You don't have to marry her," Tom said.

"What?" his father asked.

It was his stag night, of course he was going to marry her.

"Dad, if it's just the sex, you really don't have to marry her," Tom persisted. He had his reasons for being concerned. Just three hours ago he had been between her thighs, and he knew just how intoxicating she could be.

Jim looked at his son harshly, "You don't need to worry. Your inheritance is safe."

That was not what Tom was worried about, but he had no intention of telling his father about his regular encounters with his soon-to-be stepmother. He wasn't quite sure how that had all started, but he had come to realise it was all about power. He had not seen the snares she'd set to entrap him, though, looking back, they had been pretty obvious.

"I'm just looking out for you, Dad," Tom said lamely.

His father slapped him on the back, "I know you are," he said, "but I'm in control. And I know what I'm getting myself into."

"If only you did," Tom thought, "If only you did."

* * *

TOM OBSERVED the marriage ceremony and he observed the marriage as it settled into its own peculiar rhythms. His observations served only to convince him that his father had made a huge and extremely expensive mistake.

Her hold on the family business increased. It was only three years ago that she had been taken on as Jim's secretary, and now she was a full partner and was starting to call the shots.

She had secured a number of very lucrative contracts for the company and their financial situation had stabilised and moved into profit and Jim seemed to be in thrall to her for this. Tom could not deny the financial benefits of her input; he was the company accountant and he could see them on all his spreadsheets.

Their encounters continued and Tom knew only too well that he too was under her control and he hated himself for it and was powerless to refuse her.

* * *

THE AGE DIFFERENCE between them made Jim increasingly aware of his own mortality and led him to book himself a health check with the local private hospital. The results were reassuringly pleasing. He was in excellent health.

That made it all the more surprising when the dizziness began, and the extreme fatigue.

"I think we should sort out some life insurance," she said one morning at breakfast.

He looked up from his newspaper.

"Don't you feel secure enough?" he asked.

"Of course," she smiled, "but it just makes sense to me."

He looked at her, her face and hair caught by the early morning sunlight and his head told him once more that she was so exquisitely beautiful that there was no reason she should want to be with him.

"What did I do to deserve you?" he asked.

"You believed in me. "

He nodded. He did indeed see beyond her beauty and he knew what an exceptional business brain she had. "We'll get in touch with my broker," he said. "He'll sort something out."

He appreciated the care she took with their diet. All the years he had lived alone had made him lazy and he ate out far too often, ordered takeaways regularly and seldom cooked. Fruit and vegetables were alien to him. That was why he had been relieved to be given a clean bill of health when he had indulged himself with a head to toe medical screening.

She looked after herself. In many ways she was high-maintenance, with her treatments and salon appointments, but she was extremely health conscious and supervised their meals with extreme diligence. It annoyed him that as soon as he started eating healthily he started to feel unwell, and her energy smoothies, packed with vitamins, were not working.

Tom was concerned about his father. He could see he was losing weight, and occasionally he saw him having to steady himself. He mentioned it one afternoon when they were in bed in his flat.

"I know," she said. "I think he just needs a holiday, so maybe I can persuade him to take a break."

She was very persuasive and so they sorted out their travel insurance with the broker when Jim sorted out life insurance.

"Can you sort out policies for us both," Jim asked.

She looked at him in astonishment. "I thought we were just getting cover for you."

"Don't you think you're worth insuring?" he asked. "You're my most valuable asset." His loving response settled the matter and the policies were arranged.

* * *

SHE ORGANISED THEIR BREAK. They went to the Riviera. The weather was fine, the hotel was expensive and the food and wine were exquisite. Her beauty attracted attention everywhere they went, and his head told him again and again that she could not really want to be with him.

She was captivated by the boats lined up in the harbour that were for hire. She could think of nothing better than to take one out and moor it at sea over night and see the sunset over the Mediterranean and wake up to the sunrise. He was, she knew, an experienced sailor, and she set about persuading him.

He knew she was adding an extraordinarily expensive addition to their already costly break, but even he could see the special allure of a night alone out at sea.

They shopped in the market for provisions, bought lobster and langoustines from the fish stall, fruit and salad from the market and chose wine and champagne at the vintners and boarded their craft.

Neither could remember a more perfect time together. They eventually weighed anchor out of sight of the coastline and enjoyed dinner from the fresh market fare they had bought.

Their love making was more tender than they had known and afterwards they lay entwined, just taking in the soft sounds of the sea.

All of a sudden she threw back the covers and slipped from the bed. She picked up the bottle and turned and said that she was going to finish the champagne in the moonlight.

"And I need to lie here and recover," he said lazily, watching her ascend from the cabin.

Time drifted and he laid back and closed his eyes, listening to the sounds of the night. He was disturbed by a scream which was followed by a huge splash. He moved immediately, going up to the deck and treading with care in his bare feet. Peering over the side he could see her in the water. She was spread-eagled and face down.

Without hesitation, he dived into the water. It was surprisingly cold, and it took his breath. He managed to get hold of her and tow her back to the steps. It took all his strength to haul her lifeless body up the steps, and he was aware that she was crashing into them as he hauled her.

He lowered her to the deck. Choices. His mind was whirling. Summon help first then revive her? Revive then summon help?

He ran for his mobile and called for help, managing the phone with one hand whilst he checked for a pulse.

He started chest compressions and was horrified to feel her sternum crack with the pressure, but he kept pumping away. He knew the drill for CPR from the sailing courses he'd done in the past and he kept going, kept going and, at last, he heard the engine noise of an approaching craft.

The two men found a distraught, naked man working to save a beautiful woman. One took hold of him and pulled him firmly but kindly away and the other took charge of the woman.

The man did not attempt CPR. He checked for a pulse in her neck, but her body temperature and colour told him she was long dead. He shook his head at his colleague, who had found a blanket and wrapped it round Jim's shoulders.

* * *

43

TOM WENT BACK to the house with Jim after the funeral. This had been the very last outcome he had expected.

His father poured them both a drink and sat down. There was a pause before his father spoke.

"I'd like you to restore those funds she had you hide away. You found a way to make them disappear, so I imagine you can make them reappear."

Tom looked at his father in amazement.

"Did you think I didn't know about you two?" he asked.

There was another pause .

"Dad, I'm so sorry," as the words were spoken Tom realised how utterly inadequate they sounded. "I did try to warn you before you got married."

"You mean when you said if it was just the sex then I didn't need to marry her?" Jim asked. "You hardly put your cards on the table did you?"

He pulled a box from his pocket and laid it on the table.

"Did you know she was trying to poison me?"

Tom was astounded. He picked up the box and examined it.

"Of course I didn't. How did you find out?"

"It was pretty obvious something was going on when I started to feel bad after she put us on the energy drinks. I did a sweep of the house and found the pills. She'd got them off the internet, but they were labelled in my name as if I'd ordered them. I swapped them for vitamin pills."

"So that's why you were feeling rough," Tom said.

"There was still a trace of morphine in my blood when they checked me over after the incident. I told them it had been for pain relief."

"I don't understand why you're so calm," Tom said. "You know what I did. You know what she did and yet we're just sitting here having a drink. Why the hell did you marry her if you knew? "

Jim smiled. "It made it easy to get life insurance on her as soon as we were married."

"And why didn't you stop her when you knew she was trying to poison you?"

"Because, as I told you before we married, I was in control. Right from the start. And she's made me a very rich man."

He removed a coil of what looked like fine, colourless fishing line from his pocket and laid it on the table, caressing it lightly with his fingers as if it were a treasure.

"I think, apart from the dying, she really enjoyed her trip."

DAISY STITCH AND BARS OF TWIX

*Y*ou see, it all started when I tried to make some toast and the toaster wouldn't work. I thought the fuse had probably gone, so I found a screwdriver and took the plug apart. The fuse hadn't gone. It was still clearly in place, so I thought I'd better just pop it out and check it.

I used the screwdriver to give it a flick but my hand slipped, and I gashed my other hand with its pointed bit. I was pouring with blood, but I didn't panic because my neighbour is a doctor and I have him on speed dial.

He wasn't in, but his partner answered and said he'd come round and do what he could. He's actually a textile designer, so he popped over with his sewing kit. He looked at my hand and said he thought a daisy stitch would bring the edges of the wound together and a nice French knot would secure it. It seemed a good idea at the time.

Anyway, he asked me for some brandy, which I had to hand because I'd needed it for my Christmas cakes. He took a large swig, poured some on my hand and over his needle and told me to take a swig to help with the pain.

He'd got a Twix in his pocket and he gave me that to bite on whilst he stitched my hand, and I have to say it was really quite nice. I finished it off whilst he sewed me up.

He decided I needed hot, sweet tea for the shock and went to put the kettle on, but it didn't work so we decided there must be a power cut. He phoned his partner, the doctor, for advice and he said it was very important to keep warm and hydrated so we wrapped ourselves in the dog's blankets and finished off the brandy.

It was getting dark by now, so I switched the light on, which was odd because there was supposed to be a power cut. He phoned his partner for advice again, and he was jolly cross because he was in the middle of brain surgery. Anyway, he said that a circuit breaker had probably tripped, and we should go in the garage and see.

The garage door is electric, and it wouldn't open, and my neighbour said it was probably on the same dodgy circuit, so I got the key to open the door manually. We couldn't get the key in the lock. I tried a pin-the -tail on the donkey scatter-gun approach for quite some but failed to locate the key in the hole, so he tried taking a run at it like a charging knight with a lance and fell over.

In the meantime, some rotter had moved the handle on the side door, and I couldn't find it to get back in. My neigh-bour was in a heap on the floor and wanted to go home but couldn't remember where he lived. He did know that he had an awfully nice Ercol dining room suite and said that if I looked through some front windows, I'd know it at once and be able to come back and help him home, which is what I tried to do.

Someone must have called the police. The officer who turned up would not listen to my explanations. I tried to tell him why I was looking through windows, covered in blood, wrapped in a dog blanket, roaring drunk, with a lovely bit of embroidery on my left hand and chocolate all over my face but he just took me into custody.

And so, Sir, I have not been able to complete the audit you commissioned because I have been detained at her majesty's pleasure.

ALSO BY S D JOHNSON

Available on Amazon, an anthology of new poems entitled "I needed to drink tea with you." It is available in paperback or on Kindle.

These poems confront the human condition and examine our response to birth, death, consumerism, heritage and faith without flinching.

The reader is not asked to agree with the writer, but to engage with the concepts and reach a considered personal conclusion.

S D Johnson

I needed to drink tea with you.

Redemption

S.D. Johnson's eagerly awaited first novel examines one girl's fight to rebuild her life her way.

Chapter One

Judge describes rapist as an animal.

Wayne Jackson, 28, of Melbourne Street, pleaded guilty to rape and attempted murder today at Billingham Crown Court.

The judge, Alice Jefferson, described it as an evil and calculated act against a courageous young woman. She said that Jackson had behaved like an animal.

Jackson had been released on license just three days before the offence. He admitted forcing entry into the victim's flat and subjecting her to three hours of torture before raping her and leaving her for dead.

Jackson was caught through DNA traces found by forensic experts at the scene of the crime.

Jackson was detained for psychiatric reports, pending sentencing.

Margaret Astle, the local M.P., has called for an enquiry into Jackson's early release. He had been serving a ten-year sentence for aggravated burglary and the rape of a sixty-year-old woman.

Beth Anderson read the report in silence and then folded the newspaper in half and laid it down on the coffee table with precision, aligning it exactly with the edge of the table. At least he had had the decency to plead guilty and had saved her from having to give evidence.

"What are you thinking, Beth?" The doctor spoke after some moments.

"I am thinking that I don't want to talk about it or even think about it," she said. "In fact, I'd like to leave now."

It was always like this. Beth Anderson had resolutely refused to discuss what had happened to her and the impact it had had on her. She was willing to talk about the physical injuries and their treatment and progress, but she would not revisit the events of that night when she had woken to find Jackson in her room.

She had answered all the questions that the police had asked, she had complied with every request they made of her. She had undergone every test and examination they had required of her but, when every possible request had been met, she brought down a veil and refused to look back through it.

S D Johnson

Printed in Poland
by Amazon Fulfillment
Poland Sp. z o.o., Wrocław

53656359R00035